the surprise garden

by **zoe hall**

illustrated by **shari halpern**

SCHOLASTIC INC.
New York   Toronto   London   Auckland   Sydney
Mexico City   New Delhi   Hong Kong

This book was originally published by The Blue Sky Press in 1998.

ISBN 0-590-10076-9

Text copyright © 1998 by Zoe Hall
Illustrations copyright © 1998 by Shari Halpern
All rights reserved.
Published by Scholastic Inc.
SCHOLASTIC and associated logos are trademarks and/or registered trademarks of Scholastic Inc.

30 29 28 27 26 25 24 23   09 10

Printed in the United States of America   40

First Scholastic paperback printing, March 1999

Special thanks to Ted Maclin, Coordinator of the Children's Garden program at the Brooklyn Botanic Garden, for his expert advice on gardening.

Art direction by Kathleen Westray
Design by Kristina Iulo.

We're planting the seeds for a surprise garden.
Can you guess what we will grow?

We don't know.
It's a SURPRISE!

First, we use our trowel and rake
to loosen the soil.

Mom has given us each a handful
of all kinds of seeds.
Look at all the different shapes and sizes!

We poke the seeds into the soil,
one by one.
We have painted sticks different colors
to mark the different kinds of seeds.

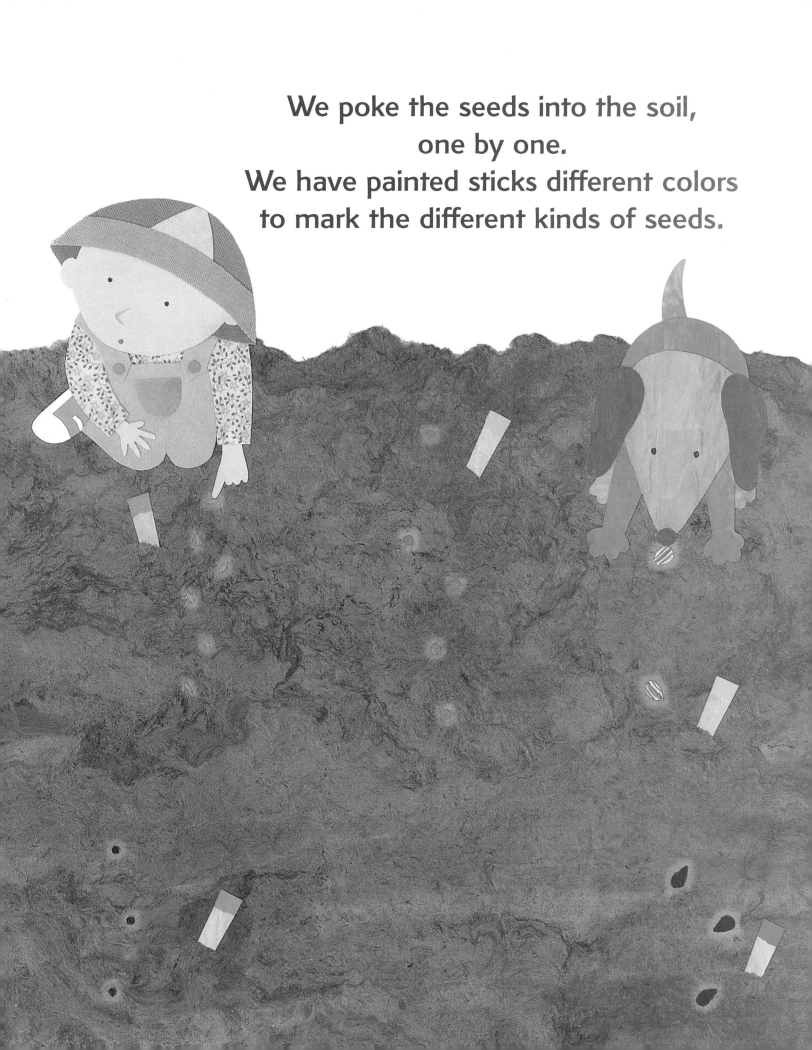

Then we water the seeds
and wait for our surprise garden to grow.

Soon, the seeds sprout into small green shoots.

We water the plants,
and the sun warms them.
Our garden grows and grows!
On some plants, flowers bloom.

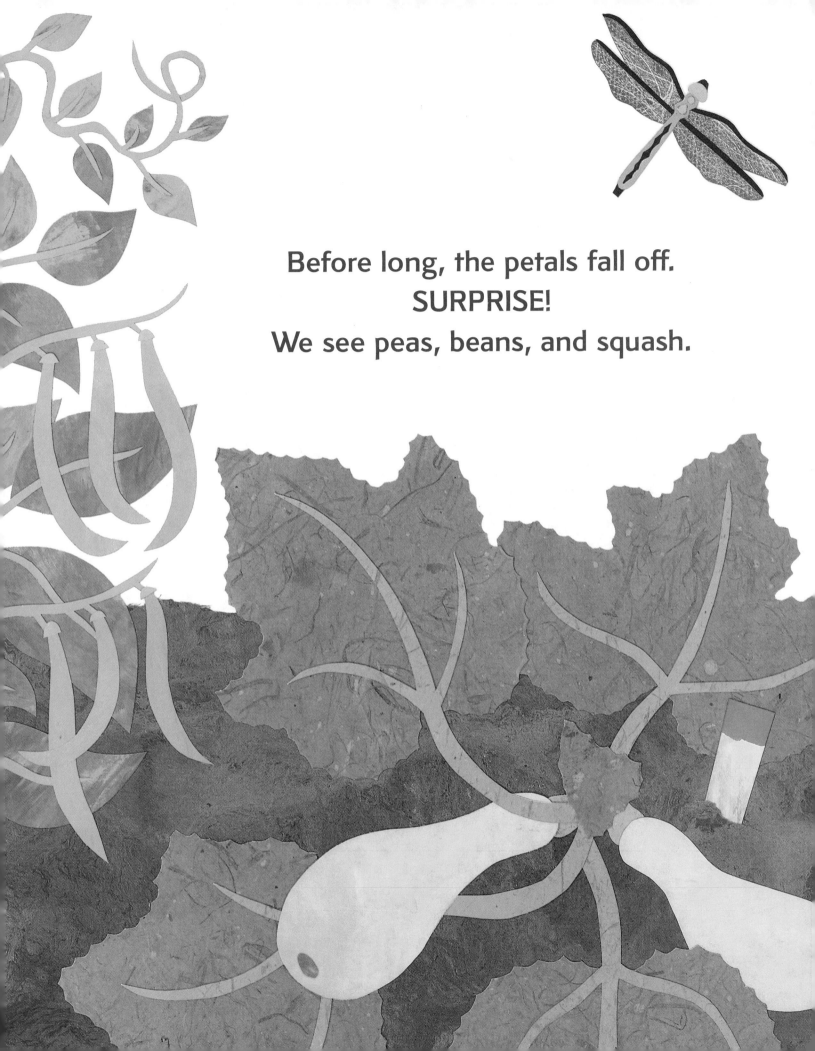

Before long, the petals fall off.
SURPRISE!
We see peas, beans, and squash.

On some plants,
leaves grow close to the ground.
SURPRISE!
We see spinach and lettuce.

And what is growing here?
SURPRISE!
We see broccoli and cauliflower.

Is anything growing here?
SURPRISE!
We find carrots and radishes.
They are growing under the ground.

Here is the longest plant in our garden.
Flowers bloomed on this plant, too.
SURPRISE!
We find a big watermelon.

Here is the tallest plant in our garden.
SURPRISE!
It's a sunflower, and it is full of tasty seeds.

All summer long,
the food in our surprise garden ripens.
We like to pick the food. . .

. . . and eat it, too!
SURPRISE!
We're having a garden party!

What we grew in our surprise garden:

These seeds grew into **pea** and **bean** plants. We eat the seeds, and sometimes the pods, of these plants.

These tiny seeds grew into **spinach** and **lettuce** plants. The leaves are good to eat.

These small seeds grew into **broccoli** and **cauliflower** plants. The parts we eat are really the flower buds.

These tiny seeds grew into **carrot** and **radish** plants. We eat the roots that grow underground.

These seeds grew into **squash** and **watermelon** plants. We eat these plants' fruits.

This striped seed grew into a tall **sunflower** plant. We eat the seeds of the flower.

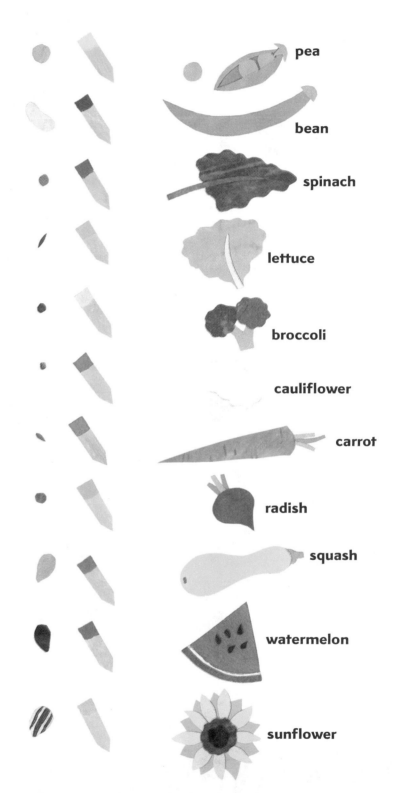

pea

bean

spinach

lettuce

broccoli

cauliflower

carrot

radish

squash

watermelon

sunflower